T0304400

WHERE

the

CANDLES

are

KEPT

McSWEENEY'S
SAN FRANCISCO

This is one in a series of stories that will, god willing, someday become something larger, called *The Forgetters*. This story, in slightly different and slightly shorter form, first appeared in *Small Odysseys*, a collection of short stories published by Selected Shorts.

Cover illustration by Angel Chang.

ISBN: 978-1-963270-03-7

These numbers could mean anything, or nothing:
10 9 8 7 6 5 4 3 2 1

www.mcsweeneys.net

Printed in Canada

WHERE

the

CANDLES

are

KEPT

by

DAVE EGGERS

For Mormor and GP

Oisín was at the airport to pick up two wayward young people, cousins to each other, grand-niece and grand-nephew to him. One was Calla, who he knew a bit. Haunted eyes, twig-thin, freckled, languid. She was probably nineteen by now, and was somehow entangled in drugs. A classmate of hers had overdosed, or almost overdosed, and Calla was involved. Or to blame. She'd thrown the party.

The other kid was Torin, a few years younger than Calla. He was what—maybe fifteen by now? Oisín remembered him from the last reunion, a shy boy, always on the periphery, his eyes watchful behind a tangle of black hair. His mother, Evie, had had a stroke three months ago, and the idea was that a month in

Idaho would help both kids. Clear their heads, give their parents some respite.

"As long as I don't have to feed them," Oisín had told their parents.

"Of course you have to feed them," their parents had said.

Eventually they agreed that Oisín would buy them food but would not cook. He didn't even cook for himself, subsisted on sandwiches and fruit and did not eat out. He loathed the concept of restaurants, serving, ordering—all the groveling and complaining and tipping. His approach was to get food, eat food, eliminating all of the attendant ceremony and supplication. This was the kind of thing the extended family expected of him, anyway—the eccentricities of an old man who lived like a woodland hermit.

"They won't have phones," Calla's mother said, and Oisín couldn't decide if that was a good thing or not. He didn't want to plan a month of activities for two LA teenagers. Had they ever seen a tree? A river unbound by concrete?

He sat at the baggage claim, nursing a dull dread. These two could be awful. They could be terrible individually and far worse together. What if they fought with each other? He hadn't heard a raised voice in years. If they quarreled, he'd send them away and burn the cabin down.

Evie had mailed him photos of Calla and Torin, and he'd brought the photos with him, like a hit man. Each plane landing at the Hailey airport only had twenty or so people on it, so he didn't think he'd have difficulty sorting the two of them out. While he waited, he flipped through a free magazine, a guide to the Wood River Valley region, and stopped at an article about the local theater group.

My God, he thought. That's her.

Fayaway Yount. He'd seen her in *As You Like It* a few years ago, the only play he'd seen since college. She was magnetic. Wry, lithe, with a mane of rich auburn hair. And the name! Fayaway. He assumed it was a stage name. Only twice had he fallen in love from afar, and each time he coveted the feeling, telling no one, forgetting nothing. The first time was with a woman crossing the street in Hartford, Connecticut, in 1989. She was in some kind of security-guard uniform, and was carrying a white umbrella in the sun.

Oisín had never married, had never been a romancer, and did not romance women now. He was seventy-two, and Fayaway Yount couldn't be more than fifty. Even the thought of it was pitiable, distasteful—his sagging, pasty flesh next to her taut olive skin. Look at that face! In the magazine, she was posing behind a rough-hewn fence, her arms resting on it in an effort to look at ease. She was wearing a kind of cowgirl outfit, brand-new, totally unconvincing and no doubt the photographer's idea. And yet her eyes bored into the viewer. They said, *I have swallowed worlds*.

"That's really my given name!" she said in the article. "They assume because I'm an actor that it's a play on Faye Dunaway. But really, my parents got it from Melville. There was a young woman in the Marquesas named Fayaway, a beautiful girl who he liked, or loved, then left. My parents liked the name more than Melville loved her, I'm guessing." The article said that Fayaway, the Idaho Fayaway, was single.

"Oisín?"

He startled and looked up. It was them. Calla was in overalls, cloth bracelets up and down her arms. Torin wore a black hoodie and long baggy shorts.

White earbuds. At least she'd said his name right. It was O-sheen, not Oy-seen.

"Good magazine?" Calla asked. "Who's the lady?"

Oisín put the magazine back in the rack, though immediately wished he hadn't. He wanted to finish the article at home, to re-read it, to have that photo of Fayaway Yount, her eyes boring into him. He grabbed the magazine, rolled it up, and put it under his arm.

"How was the flight?" he asked.

"It was a triumph," Calla said.

Torin giggled in a falsetto.

"And now I'm in Idaho," she added.

Thus far they were insufferable. With divine clarity, Oisín knew the best thing for all involved would be for the two of them to take the next plane home.

"These yours?" he asked, reaching for the two roller bags next to Calla.

"We'll get 'em," she said. "You carry your magazine."

Oisín eyed his van in the distance. He pictured driving away in it, alone. Who would fault him?

"Thank you for picking us up," Torin said.

Ah, Oisín thought. He's the polite one.

"His mom told him to always thank people at the start, like right when you get in the car," Calla said, nodding to Torin. "That way you don't forget. He told me that on the plane."

Oisín saw that Torin was horrified, as if suddenly realizing that nothing he would ever tell Calla would remain private. And then Oisín remembered something Torin's father had said. It was Calla who needed the quiet month in Idaho. Torin, a shy kid, was there as a kind of buffer. "She's a strong dose," he'd said. "If Torin comes, they can entertain each other so you don't have to."

"This is it," Oisín said when they arrived at his van. It had once belonged to an electrician friend of his. It was long and cavernous.

"Shotgun," Calla said, and then realized the van's only seating was a bench in the front. She took the seat by the window, leaving Torin in the middle. She rolled down her window and spoke to Oisín with her elbow on the window frame.

"I don't drive," she said, and looked back into the largely empty hull of the van. "But if I did, I would never drive something like this."

* * *

Torin had never really been anywhere and had never seen anything. This was the longest trip he'd ever taken, and it was just two hours by plane. He'd met Oisín twice at family reunions and had had only cursory conversations with him. He did not know or like old people, their smell and opinions, and did not look forward to spending time with this one. He was in Idaho for Calla.

"This can't be it," she said.

They were standing in front of Oisín's cabin.

"It'll be tight," Oisín said. He made a barely audible *hmm* sound, as if just now realizing he would be sharing it with two full-size people.

Torin had no reaction at all. It didn't look possible that anyone lived there, let alone that the three of them would cohabitate for the month. It was not quite a cabin. Set at the foot of a steep mountain dense with pines, it looked like the decaying dwelling of an ancient wizard. There was something about the pitched roof, crooked and covered in moss, that hinted at fading magic. A ladder leaned against its side, further confusing the geometry.

"Do you have tents?" Calla asked. "I'd almost rather stay in a tent. What about you?" She turned to Torin, who found the idea of sharing a tent with Calla intoxicating.

"I actually think you'll like it inside," Oisín said, and walked across the gravel driveway to the clearing around the cabin.

Torin followed Calla in, and the smell hit him first—pine and lacquer and the airless scent of all-day sun on old wood. The whole of the cabin was one room, about the size of a standard bedroom, with a tiny kitchen in the back that faced a narrow and winding river. The walls were cluttered with random things—old snowshoes, a photo of Roberto Clemente, and what looked like a conquistador's sword.

"Can I ask why you live out here?" Calla asked.

Torin almost laughed, because Calla's form of humor had everything to do with saying the wrong thing, and suddenly. But this time he resisted. He had no living grandparents, and had been brought up to treat the elderly with a quiet deference.

"Remember what T. E. Lawrence said about the desert?" Oisín asked. "He liked it because it was clean."

"But your place isn't clean," Calla said.

"I meant *Idaho* was clean," Oisín said. "Not my place. And my place is not *un*clean. I spent all yesterday fixing it up."

"It looks good," Torin said, and watched as Calla made a more thorough assessment.

She drew her finger across the mantle, surprised to find it free of dust. "I guess it's just cluttered. You have a lot of stuff! And all these variations on brown wood. It reminds me of an acoustic guitar. It's like living inside an acoustic guitar." She turned to Torin. "Isn't it like the inside of a guitar?"

Torin thought this analogy harmless enough. "Sort of," he said.

"And there's no bathroom?" Calla said.

They knew there was no bathroom. This had been emphasized during every mention of the summer plan. Oisín had no indoor plumbing at all. But Calla seemed to be stating this most unconscionable fact in the hope that it wasn't true.

"Follow me," Oisín said, and he led them back across the gravel drive to the outhouse, a shed, leaning left, with a moon and a trio of stars cut into its door.

Torin expected the odor to be overwhelming, but when Oisín opened the plywood door, it just smelled like more wood. There was a toilet seat embedded in a wooden shelf, and next to the seat there was a tube of hand sanitizer and a tall tower of toilet paper rolls. Each roll was as big as a spare tire.

"Got those when the bus station in Hailey ordered too many," Oisín said.

"Score," Calla said. "And look!" She pointed to a small plaque commemorating the fact that the structure had been built in 1941. "We get to shit in a historical landmark."

Torin realized then that Calla wasn't planning to stay. She would call home, make up an excuse, or flat out escape.

Oisín let the outhouse door close with a smack.

"Let's go to the lake," he said.

Calla did plan to escape. Oisín was far older than she'd remembered, and far stranger, and his cabin was not habitable. She would feel bad for Torin, would feel momentarily guilty about leaving him to the old wizard. But she couldn't take him with her. That would be kidnapping, or statutory something, and beyond that, her parents and Torin's would murder her if she made him into any kind of accomplice.

"This is the most beautiful alpine lake you'll ever see," Oisín said. They were rumbling down a two-lane highway in his rickety Unabomber bus, and cars were periodically passing them as if the van were standing still. The speed limit was sixty-five, but the van didn't seem capable of breaking fifty.

Calla had no interest in this lake. Lakes were for people who didn't live near the ocean, and alpine lakes were just lakes too cold to swim in. She had no interest in the bald black hills Oisín kept pointing to, site of this or that forest fire. *Burn, Idaho, burn*, she thought, and wished she had someone nearby who would appreciate her joke. Torin was too innocent, too good; she'd seen his face fall when she'd hazed Oisín about his filthy home.

"I rented a boat," Oisín said as they pulled into the parking lot. All around were corny log cabins and fat families waddling in the sun, carrying coolers and rafts.

"Wow," Calla said. "This is the most beautiful alpine lake I've ever seen."

11

Torin laughed; they hadn't seen the lake yet.

Oisín looked at her in a way she took to mean disappointment. Now she felt bad. He was an intriguing old guy, she thought. Not scolding. Not grumpy. There was something in his eyes, in fact, that implied he understood her sarcasm but found it unfunny.

They made their way past the main lodge, and then the vista opened up. The lake was a bright blue mirror with a jagged white mountain range at the end. It looked like a screen saver. There was a wide lawn, then a small beach bright with umbrellas and rafts, then the tiny waves of the lake rushing to the shore like mad, happy mops. A musical trio was playing something folkie on the grass, a few dozen older fans watching from folding chairs. Calla had never been to Switzerland, but her idea of Switzerland was this—everything clean and orderly and full of families in bright clothing acting appropriately and not too loud.

"I'll go deal with the boat," Oisín said, and made his way toward the dock. Calla got her first clear look at him. He wore long faded blue shorts and canvas sneakers, and walked purposefully, not at all frail. From a distance he could have been forty, fifty, the father of one of her friends.

Oisín stopped at the rental desk, around which there were a handful of pedal boats and kayaks and motorboats for rent, bobbing in the clear water. Calla thought it would be kind of fun to see what it was like out on the lake; she hadn't been in a boat in years. But then again, if she were to say she'd get seasick, she could stay on the beach while Oisín and Torin took the boat out. This would give her time to disappear. She could hitch, call an Uber, a taxi, run through the woods, anything. She'd have hours before they knew. When Oisín was out of earshot, Calla turned to Torin. "I'm leaving," she said. "I hope you understand. Obviously I can't stay."

"Leaving for where?" he asked.

"Back home, probably. I don't know. I have an aunt in Minneapolis. Maybe I go that direction."

Torin's big brown eyes were suddenly wet and red. How could he do that so quickly? She was impressed.

"I'll go with you," he said.

"You're fifteen," she said. "It'd be like kidnapping. I'd go to jail."

"I'll explain it to anyone who asks," he said in a

desperate rush. "That it was my choice. I can be useful. You're much safer if you're not alone."

This kid! Calla thought. Her cousin was in love with her, that much was obvious. "You're cute, but no," she said. "I'd get arrested. I'm nineteen, so . . ."

"You can't drive," he said. "You said so. I have my learner's permit. How will you get anywhere when you can't drive?"

Good point, she thought. "I'll hitch," she said. "My mom used to. She did it all over the country, all over fucking Greece. Apparently she was allowed to do shit like that and I'm not."

Now Oisín was walking back from the dock. He looked far older from the front, his face carved from the bark of a gnarled gray tree. He waved to them, keys in his hand.

No one knew Torin was Machiavellian, and he preferred it that way. He was a good kid who knew he was a good kid, and also knew how to use this perception to bring about events in his favor. He didn't want Calla to leave him alone with this strange old man, and he had no idea how to prevent her from leaving. For now, though, he only had to postpone her escape. He had to get her on the boat. Oisín was drawing near.

"I totally get it," he whispered to Calla, "but you can't do it now. There's nothing here. No buses, trains, taxis. There's damned sure no Ubers at this goddamned lake." Already he saw her face softening into recognition. She seemed impressed, too, by his use of "damned sure." He'd never sworn in her presence before.

"Wait till we go into town," he said. "We have to. Probably later today, for groceries. That'll be the place. Go there, get on a truck. Or catch a bus out of town. Do it there. You'll have options."

She smiled. He smiled. He'd bought at least a few hours.

When Oisín crossed the soft green lawn to get the kids, he saw her. Fayaway Yount. It was uncanny. What was she doing here? She was singing in a trio on the lawn. He hadn't known she sang, but of course all actresses sing, and of course she would be singing in a trio in a place like this. Everyone around here had four jobs. She was probably a pharmacist, too.

He moved closer to the band, and as he did, he

tuned out the squeals of children on the beach and the yaps of dogs in the shallow water. She was wearing a red linen button-down with a long white cotton skirt, and she stood barefoot, singing with her eyes closed. Somehow she was more winsome this way, in the daylight, her hair pulled back, her toes in the grass. And then her eyes opened and fell on Oisín, briefly but unmistakably, before she looked up to the sky, where the corpulent clouds pulsed with kept sun.

"It's her, isn't it?" Calla was right behind him. "I recognize her from the magazine! Jesus, Oisín, are you in love?"

Oisín was growing less fond of Calla by the minute. Torin was straightforward and shy—two admirable traits in a teenager—while this older one was acidic, maybe even cruel.

"We should get going," Oisín said. "We only have the boat for two hours." But he badly wanted to stay.

"One more song," Calla said, lowering her voice, trying to contain her glee. "Seriously. I didn't mean to be annoying. If you like her, you know, *music*, then we should stay." She was trying to suppress a grin.

"We're going," Oisín said.

Calla and Torin followed him up the narrow dock and to the boat he'd rented. He glanced one more time toward Fayaway. He decided he didn't care that Calla knew he found Fayaway intriguing. She was somehow both statuesque and cute, and she sang in a gorgeous low mezzo-soprano, like the rush of a shallow river, but he had no intentions beyond listening to her. He loved beauty, needed to always be near beauty, and when an unusual beauty was near, he found himself gripped, immobilized. It had always been this way. But he'd never needed to possess this beauty. Nearness was always enough.

Calla was giddy. She'd correctly diagnosed the crush of a seventy-two-year-old man on a fifty-year-old woman. Yes! It was adorable, and now she wondered if she really could leave when such delicious work was to be done here, and she was the only one to do it.

She followed Oisín to the small aluminum motorboat at the end of the dock. Silver and dented, it looked like it had brought army soldiers to shore in a previous century. Two teenage boys, a year or two younger than Calla, showed them the mechanical fea-

tures of the boat, handed them vests, and then stood
on the dock, inspecting Calla's shape from behind,
their wraparound sunglasses giving them cover.

Oisín dropped their bag into the boat with a dull
thump and started the engine. Torin sat dutifully by
his side and Calla took the bow. They puttered
through the no-wake zone, dodging candy-colored
kayaks and paddleboards, and when they passed the
last buoy, Oisín put the base of his hand to the throttle. They gained speed and unzipped the lake length-
wise. They sped toward the Sawtooth Mountains,
which rose from the glassy surface of the lake like tall
gray men in white shawls. In the middle of the lake, a
mile from the dock where they'd launched, Oisín cut
the engine and turned to them.

"So which of you had the pills again?" he asked.

Calla was too startled to answer. How did he know
this? He seemed like the kind of aloof older relative
who would never know or care about such details.

"I had some friends over," she said. "They found
a prescription bottle in the garbage that had some
pills still in it. You know Dilaudud?"

"Dilau*did*," Oisín corrected.

"Okay, Dilau*did*," she said. "That just started things. They found more pills upstairs. I helped, actually. We got giddy and stupid."

Calla did not expect him to be scandalized. She'd heard stories about Oisín. He'd been a hippie, and a soldier, and a hermit. He'd worked as a welder, a long-haul trucker, a river guide. She was unsure what would shock him. For the time being, he simply stared at the water as she spoke.

"I'd stashed a few bottles of champagne from Christmas," she said. "So we had a party, and everyone got sick, and one girl got scared and called her mom, and she ended up getting her stomach pumped even though she'd taken less than anyone else. The rest of us—someone should have died."

"*Could* have died," Oisín said.

"*Could* have died, fine," Calla said.

"Not *should* have died," he said, turning back to her. "Don't say *should* have."

"Okay, okay," Calla said. She didn't know what to do with his attention focused on her like this. She found it disorienting, annoying, thrilling.

"I say random things," she said. "It's my ADHD."

Oisín looked at her. "Who said you have ADHD?"

"My guidance counselor. She—"

"Is she a doctor?"

"No. But my friend who has it said that I—"

"Calla, in the past few years, there is no one I have met, no one I know—no one in my life, of any age, without exception—who has not declared themselves to have ADHD. What does that tell you?"

"That there's an ADHD epidemic?"

"No. It tells you that there is a bullshit epidemic. Your mind wanders, so you have ADHD? You sometimes have trouble concentrating, so you have ADHD? You think wandering minds are new to the human animal? Calla—and this goes for you, too, Torin—you should not *want* to be a patient. For thousands of years, people were hell-bent to stay *out* of hospitals, and away from diagnoses. Now healthy kids like you rush to apply every new clinical term to yourselves. Your parents told me that you have no conditions, and you came to stay with me without any medicines. So you aren't ADHD or anything else. You're healthy humans and you're lucky to be that way. Leave the diagnoses and doctors to the people who really need help. When healthy people go to the doctor every time they're nervous or distracted, it gums up the whole system."

"Jesus," Calla said.

"Are you hearing me, Torin?" Oisín said. A diagonal line had appeared on Oisín's forehead—from his temple to his eyebrow, a slash of mental exertion.

"Yes," Torin said.

"Don't be a patient unless you have no choice," Oisín said.

They hadn't dropped an anchor, so the gentle current was pushing them toward the shore, where a tangle of downed pines were wedged between a trio of boulders. The wind picked up.

"And Torin, I'm sorry about your mom," Oisín said. Coming from anyone else, pivoting so quickly from one familial catastrophe to the next, it would have sounded false and perfunctory. But Oisín made it sound dignified and inevitable. "I know she'll get better. She's strong."

"Thanks," Torin said.

"When she was a girl, she went up Mount Lassen

with me and Patrick. She must have been ten. In sandals! And she never complained. She ran most of the way. She ever tell you that?"

"I think so," Torin said, though he had no recollection of a story like that. His mother was what to Oisín? Niece? Something about the story unsettled him. Was it the kind of thing you said about someone dead or dying? Every day since her stroke, Torin flung himself between defending her and being disgusted by her—half her face fallen, numb, her constant drooling, the thick-tongued way she spoke now.

He was avoiding Oisín's eyes, looking into the lake, which had appeared much smaller from the dock but now seemed vast. The silver mountains that rose up from the lake's end were closer now, but still seemed miles away. Then he saw something on the surface. It was white, lumpy. It looked like a diaper.

"Look," he said, relieved to change the subject.

"Huh," Oisín said. "You never see garbage on this lake. See if you can grab it."

Torin reached down to get it. The diaper was heavy with lake water. He dropped it onto the boat floor with a wet slap.

"There's a whole bunch of stuff over here," Calla said. She was leaning over the other side of the boat. "A sandal. A bag of chips. Oh shit, a life preserver."

There was a dark snakelike object that Torin took to be a shirt. A Styrofoam cooler, open, with an apple core inside. A plastic water bottle, half-full. It was as if someone had dumped the contents of a beach bag into the lake.

"Grab as much as you can," Oisín said.

"What do you think happened?" Calla asked.

"Looks like it fell off a boat," Oisín said. "Maybe they were going fast and didn't realize they'd lost this stuff."

Torin reached for a pink sweater wound around a life vest. He dropped it onto the floor of the boat.

"Over here," Calla said, and grabbed a plastic carton of baby wipes. "Why is there a diaper and wet wipes? I'm freaking out now."

Torin's heart hammered. He scanned the water, expecting to see a baby.

"Look!" Calla yelled. "Bonnet! Baby bonnet!" She held it up, horrified, flinging it back into the water. "What the fuck is all this?"

"Calm down," Oisín said.

Torin was still leaning over the edge, reaching for a pair of goggles, when he saw, a few feet under the surface, the ghostly silver triangle of the bow of a boat.

Oisín rushed to Torin's side. The bow was sticking straight up. To be positioned that way, and with all their possessions still close, the sinking must have been recent.

"Look for people," he said evenly.

"People? Where?" Calla cried.

Oisín searched the shoreline, hoping to find a family shivering there. He could see one of the smaller campsite beaches, not more than two hundred yards away. There were a few families lounging in the shallows, oblivious. Whoever had been in this boat was not on shore. Which meant they were still inside the boat. But none of this made sense. A single boat, sunk in twenty feet of water? And no one else near?

Oisín was staring down, furious at himself that he hadn't already jumped in, when he heard a splash. He turned to see Calla's ankles disappear.

* * *

Calla had not thought it through, had not guessed how cold and hard the water would be. It was like breaking through plate glass. Immediately she was at the sunken boat, her arm buckling; it was so close she'd struck it at nearly full force. She felt its smooth silver bow and took the railing and pulled herself down the side, hand over hand. She saw no people. The boat was the same kind Oisín had rented. It had no cabin. She wanted no cabin. A cabin could mean there were people trapped inside—a baby even. Where was the baby?

A hand gripped her calf. She screamed underwater. A second hand appeared in front of her and she screamed again. Finally she saw a face. It was Oisín.

He'd taken off his shirt and jumped in after her, and thought he should let her know he was there, too, so she wouldn't be startled. But his plan had produced the opposite effect. She panicked, roared underwater in a burst of manic bubbles, and was now out of breath.

He saw her point herself toward the surface and kick her way up to the light. Oisín's own lungs were on fire. He had about thirty seconds of air left, so he grabbed the windshield of the boat and used it to pull himself downward.

There was nothing visible, nothing but a towel tied to the stern. He pulled himself farther down, determined to reach the outboard motor, thinking there was a chance that someone was stuck underneath. The boat could have hit chop, gone airborne, flipped, sunk.

He pulled himself down, hand over hand on the side rail, until he was at the bottom. The water was thick with sand and muck, everything gray and green. He saw nothing near the motor. Whatever had happened to the people on this boat, they were no longer here.

Just as he was ready to return to the surface, he heard a dull crash above, and looked up to see Torin's body like an arrow, shooting downward.

Calla had flung herself up from the lake and was gasping, holding on to the back ladder. "Go check on him," she'd said, and Torin had thrown off his shirt and dove, finding himself instantly at the bottom of the lake.

Oisín was struggling under the boat. It looked like a tug-of-war, with Oisín violently pulling away from

the outboard. Torin swam closer and waved to Oisín.
Oisín pointed to his shorts, which were tangled in the
motor's propeller. Torin tried to unweave the fabric
but it was no use, Oisín's struggling had drawn it too
taut. Torin began instead to pull down on the shorts,
with the aim of taking them off completely.

Oisín understood. He fumbled at the drawstring
but it wouldn't give. Torin needed scissors or a blade.
Oisín could die this way, Torin thought—this old man
could die while trying to untie his shorts. But then he
did it, Oisín loosened the knot. Torin pulled down,
the shorts went slack, and Oisín went free and upward. Torin followed.

Calla was in the boat, pulling Oisín by the armpits,
trying to get his old naked body out of the water.
"Push from below!" she yelled to Torin, who was still
in the lake, gasping and coughing.

Torin put his shoulder under Oisín's thighs and
pushed. Calla pulled. He was too heavy.

"Again!" she demanded.

Torin went under again, and again thrust upward,
and this time Oisín seemed to awaken, and his arms

rose and he gripped Calla's, and she threw herself backward into the boat, and Oisín fell next to her. A weak gasp emerged from him, but then he went silent.

Torin climbed in and stood over Oisín, his naked body bony and blue. Torin thought of Picasso's old blue guitarist. "Oisín?" he said. "Oisín?" Torin crouched close to him and grabbed his wrist. "How do you do the pulse? The pulse-checking?"

"I don't know!" Calla said.

"He's so cold."

"Of course he's cold! We have to get back."

Now the sky was a low iron ceiling. The sun was gone, the wind was slashing.

"You drive," she said.

"I don't know how to drive a boat!" he said.

"It's the same!" she yelled. "Try the key at least."

Torin turned the key in the ignition, and it started just like a car. He looked at the handle next to the steering wheel. There was room for it to be pushed forward, so he pushed it forward. The engine grunted and the boat lurched ahead.

"Good," Calla said. "Now turn the fuck around."

Torin turned the steering wheel and the boat followed suit. It was the same as a car. There was nothing different. He could steer it, they would make it back. But stopping? He didn't know about stopping.

"Good," Calla said again. "Now faster."

He pushed the throttle farther toward the dashboard. The boat roared and the wake gnashed. They raced across the lake and toward the dock.

Calla put Oisín's and Torin's shirts on top of him and propped his head on the wet sweater they'd pulled from the lake. Oisín's mouth was forming words, but he said nothing.

Close to shore, while Torin steered, Calla waved her arms wildly. She wanted people to worry, to panic, to scream. She got the attention of the two boys working at the dock. They ran to the closest slip and began guiding Torin in.

"Cut the engine! Cut the engine!" they yelled. Torin didn't know what that meant.

"Turn the key in the ignition," Oisín said. "Left." He lay in the back of the boat, Torin's T-shirt draped over his midsection. Calla was startled to hear him speak. She'd assumed he was dying or dead.

Torin turned the key left. The engine died. They drifted into the dock. One of the dock boys jumped into their boat and steered it into a slip.

"Is he dead?" he asked, staring at Oisín's blue face.

"Just cold," Oisín said.

Calla jumped from the boat. A young couple was getting out of another rental and she pulled their towels from their shoulders. "Need these!" she said, and ran back to Oisín. She put one towel under his head and the other over his waist. His skin ivory and blue, his legs entwined, he looked like an aging Jesus pulled down from the cross.

"Can you sit up?" she asked.

"In a minute," he said. "Tell them about the capsized boat."

"We saw a boat," Torin said. "Sunk. On the other end of the lake, by the mountains. You know anything about it?"

"Shit," one of the boys said.

"What?" Calla asked. "What? What?"

"It's fine," the boys said. "It sunk yesterday. Everyone's fine. I knew we should have grabbed all that stuff." He looked accusatorily at the other dock boy.

"What about the baby?" Calla asked.

"The baby wasn't on the boat," the boy said. "It was my aunt who rented the boat. The baby wasn't there. They left the baby on shore."

"Goddamnit!" Calla yelled. She knew she should be happy that the baby was fine, had never been in danger, but still she was apoplectic. "Shit-fuck!" she yelled. "Fuck-fuck-fuck!"

Oisín laughed hoarsely. "They left the baby on shore," he said, and then passed out.

Oisín couldn't get warm. He'd been brought into the lodge and installed in a giant leather chair by the fireplace, but he couldn't stop shaking. The lodge's staff huddled around him, laid blankets upon blankets on him, started a fire for him, in the middle of June.

Calla wanted to call the paramedics, but Oisín refused. He begged Calla and Torin and the lodge manager, Carmen, not to call anyone. He'd walked himself off the boat, he noted, off the dock, across the beach, and into the lodge, talking all the while. He did not need a hospital, he said. He needed to catch his breath, stare at the fire, get warm.

Soon the staff floated away, watching him from across the amber-colored room, leaving him to Calla and Torin. The teenagers were sitting on the fireplace hearth, their backs to the fire, talking to Oisín, watching him warily. "Don't worry," he told them.

Oisín was worried. Not worried, perplexed. He'd been inside the lodge for thirty minutes and was still shivering uncontrollably. The lake had been cold, but it was the naked ride back that had done it. The wind had cut through him, made him feel featherlight and porous. If not for that ride back, with that icy wind, he would be okay.

Now he was fighting violent chills. Just when he muffled one, another came on. He looked at the clock. Four thirty. If he wasn't better by five he'd let the kids call a doctor. But a doctor meant the horrifying embarrassment of an ambulance, and then a hospital, and a paper gown, and a building full of infections, and everyone he knew—everyone his age who'd gone in— had never come out.

At six, just as the dinner rush began to crowd the lodge, Oisín's chills subsided and he said he wanted to go home. Torin drove.

They had to sneak out of the lodge, really, for otherwise there would have been questions. *Aren't you too young to drive? Where are you all going? Are you sure he's okay? What's your address, your phone number, so we can check up on him?*

Oisín was leaning against the passenger-side window, wearing sweatpants and wool socks and a knit cap and a hoodie, all donated by the lodge's gift shop. There were no turns on the road from the lake to Oisín's cabin, so Torin kept his hands at ten and two, feeling godlike, urgent, Calla's bare thigh against his.

In the morning, Calla felt sure that Oisín might die. She and Torin were outside the cabin, debating next steps. They'd been up all night, taking turns watching him, feeling his forehead, covering him with every blanket and sheet in the cabin. They'd wrapped his feet in wool ski hats.

"He's like eighty," she said. "At that age, anything goes. They get a cold and then they're dead. He's still clammy and feverish."

"Then let's call the hospital," Torin said.

"No hospital," she said. "But I bet we can find a doctor."

Oisín lay inside, on his bed, hearing their muffled conversation, very much amused. He was not close to death, and had told them this all through the night, whenever they checked on him.

He was sure they hadn't slept. Each time he woke up, one of them was by his side, sitting on the hard Quaker chair he used to stack kindling. One time he woke to find Calla holding his hand, the bones in her knuckles so smooth and so cold, like river stones. Another time he found Torin standing on the other side of the room, hands behind his back, looking out the window like a general before battle. All along, the room had been illuminated by candles. How had they found the candles? Even he didn't know where he stored the candles.

And now it was morning and Oisín felt much better, was hungry, in fact, and these two teenagers were outside, considering his imminent death.

It was Torin's idea to return to the lake. By midmorning, Oisín seemed far better. His face had gone from gray to pink and his temperature seemed close to normal, but it would not hurt to bring a doctor back to the cabin. Calla had convinced Torin that a hospital was out of the question—it was against Oisín's wishes. But going to the lake and bringing a doctor back, they agreed, would not violate any pact. The lake was close enough, and full of people, and surely one of them was a doctor or nurse.

"And it's the only place we know how to get to," Calla said. She looked at him flatly, and Torin had the vague feeling she wanted him to say no.

"Okay," he said, and they left.

Torin drove with arms stiff, breathing tensely through his nose, occasionally glancing at the sky, the mountains, the half-burned forests all around them. After a few miles, Torin felt Calla's eyes on him.

"You're doing good, Torin," she said.

This was the first time Calla had said Torin's name, but it was the third time she'd complimented him that day, and he wanted to thank her, to look over to her and smile and tell her that he'd never felt stronger. And that he loved her. No. Not that. Not in

35

a romantic way, but in a way that meant he would stand by her for all their days, as friend or guardian, together or apart, as cousins and allies. He'd fly across the world to defend her.

He wanted to say all this to Calla, but then realized that a hero would not go on and on like that, not now. A hero, complimented this way, would simply nod and stare at the road ahead. So he simply nodded and stared at the road ahead.

"You think he'll die?" Calla asked.

"No," Torin said. But then he wasn't sure.

"I wouldn't want to be there if he did. If he's dying right now, I'm glad we're out here. I don't want to see it happen."

Torin pictured Oisín taking a last breath, and then having to do that thing where you close the eyes of the dead. He didn't want to touch a dead man, but he did want to close his eyes. That part had always seemed noble and right.

He wanted Calla to come and see his mom. She would know how to talk to his mom, would give him a new way to see his mother after her stroke—some practical and breezy way to see his mother with her slurred speech and half-paralyzed face. Calla would tell him how to be, what to say, how to stare straight at her.

When they arrived at the lake, immediately Calla felt silly. How would they find a doctor? They couldn't go to Carmen, the lodge manager, and ask who among their guests was a doctor. Carmen would know what was up and would call an ambulance. Walking the beach asking for a doctor would have the same effect. There would be inquiries and fuss. Cops.

"This won't work," Calla told Torin.

"Don't quit yet," Torin said.

"Excuse me?" Calla said. She was outraged at his impertinence.

"Give it a second," Torin said.

"Fuck you, 'Give it a second,'" she said.

He was right. She knew it. She just didn't want more cops. The cops who had come to her house were so condescending. One minute she'd been Calla, a radical human with many ideas and friends and above-average grades at a very good school, but to the cops, who had been all over her house in their giant black costumes, all their bulk, all their tools, she was an imbecile. Flighty, irresponsible—a stupid adolescent who did the usual stupid things. The predictability of the party, the drugs they'd found, the almost-overdosing—that bothered her more than anything.

"Such a cliché," that one lady cop had said. She was about fifty, probably a mother herself. The word had shocked Calla. What kind of person would say that word, *cliché*, while paramedics were wheeling Lily away on a stretcher? It wasn't the time for that word. After Lily got better, for weeks and then months all Calla could think about were those words, *Such a cliché*, defining her totality.

"Look," Torin said. He pointed to a woman on the grass. It was the actress. She was singing in her band again, on the wide lawn with the jagged mountains behind her.

"Let's ask her to come back with us," Calla said.

Torin thought Calla had lost her mind. They'd come to get a doctor but were bringing home a singer?

"Let's at least ask her," Calla said. "If he's not dead it'll give him reason to live."

"I won't do it," Torin said.

But Calla would. There were certain species of adults who were intimidating, but hippie singers in Idaho were not among them. Calla waited till the end of the band's set, which might have been cut short because she was lingering in front, staring at Fayaway with unsettling intensity.

"We need a favor," Calla said.

It was not a bother for Fayaway. Unusual, yes, but not so unusual for this region. She'd been living in this part of Idaho on and off for thirty years, and she'd met more than a few off-grid oddballs. One noted hermit, Salmon River Sal, had come to a production of *Three Days of Rain* on three consecutive nights. He had introduced himself politely afterward, and she had never heard from him again. Some years later, she read that he'd died in his lair. Among his few belongings was a program from the play, her name underlined every time it appeared.

So this did not seem so different. The two kids acting as intermediaries was a new one, but otherwise she was accustomed to the attention of older men, gentlemanly men who rarely wanted anything more than a moment's proximity.

She was surprised when the younger, smaller one got into the driver's seat of the long white van—the girl was taller, seemed older and more capable. But Fayaway got into her truck and followed them the twenty miles to the old man's cabin. It was this kind of thing that had brought her, and kept her, in these small towns, these jumbled Idaho towns that looked like they'd rolled down the mountains to settle like stones on the valley floor.

Through the van's rear windows, she watched the two kids, the backs of their heads as they looked steadily at the winding road ahead. Such purpose! At the lodge, she'd taken them to be the same kind of listless, scowling teens that her friends had produced, but then they had laid out their request and provided a short biography of their uncle, or great-uncle, and their vision seized her. This kind of thing never happened in the suburbs of Atlanta where she was raised. Only in the emptiness of Idaho could you see people one by one, and breathe a bit, and ask a favor like this. She felt at home in their dream.

*   *   *

Oisín was in his cabin, in his bed, awake and feeling fine. Earlier, he'd gotten up, fixed himself a bowl of mush and changed into his own clothes. That task had tuckered him out, though, so when he heard the van pull up, spitting gravel and stopping in a rush of white dust, he was reclining again, covered in a light wool blanket. There was no window that faced the driveway, so he couldn't see them coming in, but he heard a solicitousness in the voices of the kids that was new. Then he heard a third voice, flutelike, almost familiar.

The door opened and Torin's face appeared, his brow furrowed, apologetic. Calla followed, chin up, grinning, eyes alight.

"You look good!" she said. She seemed surprised.

"You do," Torin said. "And you changed clothes."

"I am good," Oisín said. "And I did change."

Calla walked over and pressed the back of her hand to Oisín's forehead. "No fever," she said.

"We brought someone," Calla said.

"It's not a doctor," Torin said.

"Or a priest," Calla added.

Oisín laughed, and Calla nodded to whoever was

just beyond the open door. Then Fayaway Yount stepped through, from the brightness outside and into his cabin. Fayaway was in his home, and immediately he saw it through her eyes. He was an animal living in a cave, a burrow. He watched as she looked around briefly, her eyes adjusting to the darkness and the clutter, and then she found him, the old man in the corner. She smiled and came to him.

"How are you?" she asked, sitting in the hard Quaker chair. She was gorgeous up close, far more radiant than onstage or in any photo. Everything about her, even the whites of her eyes, was polished bright.

She stayed for ten minutes or so, looking at Oisín like a nurse, as if she were playing a nurse—a nurse who knew just the effect she had on the men in her care. There was nothing in her demeanor that said she would ever consider Oisín a man for her to kiss and love, but still, he adored her for coming all this way. For following these two teenagers to him. Oisín looked over her shoulder and found them, Calla and Torin. They had become a kind of parental couple, leaning into each other as they watched, hoping they'd done something right.

There is still courage among us, Oisín thought. It only has to be brought forth. From the depths of our slippery and selfish selves, it has to be conjured, called upon. These two kids, who had seemed to him so flimsy yesterday, turned out to be monumental. They had gorgeous butterfly hearts beating hard within ribs of gold, and they could be trusted with the world.

DAVE EGGERS is the author of *The Eyes & the Impossible*, *The Monk of Mokha*, and *The Circle*, among other books. He is based in the San Francisco Bay Area.

NOTES & ACKNOWLEDGMENTS

This book was first published by Selected Shorts and Algonquin Books, in an anthology celebrating the thirty-fifth anniversary of Selected Shorts. Their indefatigable work celebrating and amplifying the art of the short story cannot be overpraised. We must protect them.

That collection, *Small Odysseys*, was edited by the great Hannah Tinti. Thank you, my friend, for making this story far better than when you found it.

Where the Candles Are Kept is part of *The Forgetters* series of mini-books. If all goes according to plan, these standalone stories will someday be part of a larger work. Exactly when this will happen, no one knows.

Thank you for early reads and help along the way: Amanda Uhle, Amy Sumerton, and VV. Thank you also to cover artist Angel Chang, and to copy editors Caitlin Van Dusen and Emily Lang.

Author proceeds from this book go to McSweeney's
Literary Arts Fund, helping to ensure the survival
of nonprofit independent publishing.

www.mcsweeneys.net

McSweeney's, founded in 1998, amplifies original voices
and pursues the most ambitious literary projects.

WE PUBLISH:

McSweeney's Quarterly Concern, a journal of new writing

The Believer magazine, featuring essays, interviews, and columns

Illustoria, an art and storytelling magazine for young readers

McSweeneys.net, a daily humor website

An intrepid list of fiction, nonfiction, poetry, art and
uncategorizable books, including the Of the Diaspora
series—important works of twentieth-century
literature by Black American writers